Sherman the Sheep

Dave and Pat Sargent are longtime residents of Prairie Grove, Arkansas. Dave, a fourth-generation dairy farmer, began writing in early December 1990, and Pat, a former teacher, began writing shortly after. They enjoy the outdoors and have a real love for animals.

Sherman the Sheep

By

Dave and Pat Sargent

Illustrated by
Jeane Huff

Ozark Publishing, Inc.
P.O. Box 228
Prairie Grove, AR 72753

Library of Congress cataloging-in-publication data

Sargent, Dave, 1941—
    Sherman the sheep / by Dave and Pat Sargent ;
illustrated by Jeane Huff.
        p. cm.
    Summary: A young lamb who whines and cries
    about everything wanders off from the flock as they
    are going to their summer pasture and is stlaked by
    wild animals. Includes facts about sheep.
    ISBN 1-56763-392-7   (hardcover). — ISBN 1-
56763-393-5   (pbk)
    [1.Sheep—Fiction.   2. Lost children—Fiction.]
    I. Sargent, Pat, 1936—   .
    II. Huff, Jeane, 1946—   ill. III. Title.
    PZ7.S2465Sh   1998   97-26506
    [Fic]—dc21   CIP
                                            AC

Copyright © 1998 by Dave and Pat Sargent

Printed in the United States of America

iv

Inspired by

a little lamb we had on the farm.

Dedicated to

those who have been lost and scared.

Foreword

Sherman is a young sheep who whines and cries about every little thing. He is a crybaby. When he decides to leave his summer pasture and the rest of the flock and go back home, he gets lost. He is hungry and scared and hears eerie howls. When the wild animals pick up his trail, he really has something to cry about.

Contents

One	Shearing Time	1
Two	The Summer Pasture	11
Three	Sherman Learns a Lesson	25
Four	Sheep Facts	33

Sherman the Sheep

If you would like to have the authors of the Animal Pride Series visit your school, free of charge, call 1-800-321-5671 or 1-800-960-3876.

One

Shearing Time

It was early spring, and the weather was getting very warm. It was time for all the sheep to get their wool sheared. The sheep were put in the corral, and one by one, they were led into the barn where their wool was cut off with a pair of clippers.

When the sheep came out of the barn, they looked funny and everyone laughed. The sheared sheep laughed back and said, "Just wait. Your turn is coming."

Sherman, one of the young

lambs, did not want his wool cut. He started whining to his mama. She said, "It will be all right, Sherman. All sheep have to get sheared every spring. If they don't get sheared, they will get too hot during the summer."

Being too hot didn't really matter to Sherman. He did not want his wool cut off. So, he kept whining.

When it was Sherman's turn to get sheared, he threw a big fit—a conniption fit! He whined and cried and bawled the entire time his wool was being sheared.

After every sheep and lamb was sheared, Sherman looked all around. He was surprised to see that everyone looked the same. Sherman wasn't mad anymore. He had been afraid he would look funny and that everyone else would make fun of him.

The sheep and lambs found that they could run faster and jump higher without all that heavy wool to carry around, so they ran and jumped and played all day.

A week after all the sheep and lambs had been sheared, it was time for them to be moved to their summer home. The older sheep knew that it would take about two days for them to walk to their summer pastures. But it would be worth the long walk.

Their summer home was a nice place nestled back in the hills. There would be lots of green grass and a cool breeze blowing off the mountains.

This was the first time for the little lambs to go to the summer pastures. They were all excited about going, that is, all but Sherman. He started whining and crying. He didn't want to go. Sherman wanted to spend the summer right where he was.

Bright and early the next morning, the sheep and lambs were rounded up and headed out for the hills and their summer home. Sherman whined and cried all day. All the other lambs were running and jumping and having a great time along the way. This was their very first time away from the barnyard pasture, and they were excited about all the new things they were seeing.

Late that evening, just before sundown, the sheep were bedded down for the night. They were very tired from walking all day, and it wasn't long until they were sound asleep; that is, all but Sherman. The poor little lamb was lying there beside his mama, whimpering and whining. He wanted to go back to the barnyard pasture.

All day long, the sheep had told Sherman they were going to a much better place to spend the summer,

but Sherman didn't care. He just lay there and thought about how he could get back to the barnyard pasture. It was way late in the night before he finally fell asleep.

Two

The Summer Pasture

The very next morning at the crack of dawn, all the sheep were rousted out of bed. They got up and stretched and yawned and started grazing. They were allowed to graze for about an hour before they were headed out for the summer pasture.

Again, little Sherman started whimpering and whining. All the sheep ignored him. He was just a big crybaby, and they knew that once they got to the summer pasture, everything would be all right, and

Sherman would stop being a cry-baby.

It was going to be another long

day for the sheep, for they would not arrive at the summer pasture until late afternoon, just in time to eat before it got dark.

As the sun eased below the horizon and darkness covered the sky, all the sheep bedded down for the night.

Sherman was still not happy. He wanted to go back to the barn-yard pasture. He decided to leave the flock and find his way back.

After the sheep were sound asleep, Sherman quietly slipped away from the flock and headed down the hill toward the farm. There was only a quarter moon, and it didn't give much light, so it was hard for him to find the trail.

Unaware of all the dangers which lay ahead, young Sherman

continued on. He had traveled only a short way from the flock when he heard the scary sound of a coyote howling somewhere in the distance. His mama had told him that coyotes love the taste of sheep, especially tender lambs.

Sherman's mama had told him that coyotes never bother a large flock, but they always look for stray sheep or little lambs that wander away from the herd.

And now Sherman heard wolves howling nearby. The howls of the wolf pack scared him, and he started running. He ran and ran as fast as he could. He ran until he could run no more. Then he stopped.

Sherman looked all around. He could not see the trail. With all the fast running he had done, he had gotten off the beaten path.

Sherman lay down to rest, but as soon as his tired body hit the ground, the wolves began howling again. And, this time, they were close by. His only thought was to hide. He quickly looked around. He saw a clump of cedars near him. He crawled underneath one that had been broken over by an ice storm that had occurred during the winter.

Sherman didn't know that wolves and coyotes had a keen sense of smell and that if they ever got downwind from him, they could pick up his scent and would get him for sure.

Poor Sherman, too scared to move, closed his eyes and lay waiting, completely motionless, under the broken clump of cedar.

The wolves were so close that Sherman could hear them walking through the leaves just a few feet away. He thought they were up-wind from him and could not smell him. But then they began whining real low. He knew what this meant. It meant they had picked up his scent. He squenched his eyes tight and waited.

Finally, Sherman decided to run. He opened his eyes and looked around, trying to figure out which direction to go. He could see the wolves just a few feet away. Just as he started to stand up and run, a great big ole jack rabbit jumped out

from under a nearby bush and took off just as fast as it could run, and the wolf pack was right behind it.

So Sherman was spared, at least for the moment. He stayed under the clump of cedars until it was light the next morning.

As the sun started creeping from below the eastern horizon, Sherman crawled out from under the cedars where he had been hiding.

He had changed his mind about going back to the barnyard pasture. For the first time in his life he knew what it was like to be alone. It was not a good feeling. There was no one to talk to.

Sherman was very hungry and decided to find some grass to eat before trying to find his way back to the summer pasture where he had left the others. He remembered seeing lots of lush green grass on the way to the summer pasture, but now all he could find were trees and leaves all over the ground.

Sherman kept searching for something to eat. He searched all day but found nothing. The sun was sinking low in the sky, and Sherman knew it would be dark soon. He remembered the night before when the wolves had almost gotten him, and he started getting scared. He didn't know what to do.

As the sun began to set, the wolves began to howl, and then, the coyotes started howling. Sherman was so scared! He knew he must find a safe place to hide for the night. He looked and looked for such a place, but not one place could he find.

Sherman began to cry, but his crying did no good. There was no one to feel sorry for him. Being a crybaby was not going to help Sherman, not this time.

The sky grew even darker. It would soon be too dark to see. The only thing he could find was a pile of leaves which had been piled up by the wind against an old dead log.

Sherman crawled into the leaves and lay down. He was so tired he could hardly keep his eyes open, but he was so scared he couldn't sleep.

Sherman lay there for hours listening to the wolves and the coyotes howling, and all the time, he sobbed. He wished he had never run away. Then, he thought about all of his friends and how much he wanted to be with them. Suddenly, Sherman's thoughts were interrupted by the rattling of leaves.

Three

Sherman Learns a Lesson

Instantly, Sherman was alert. His eyes opened wide, and his ears perked up. What could it be? He

slowly turned his head back and forth, unable to see very well through the thick trees. Then, he spotted the outline of an animal only a few yards away.

As the animal inched closer, Sherman could see that it was a lone coyote. He froze. He thought that maybe he would be lucky like he had been the night before. But the coyote had picked up Sherman's scent and was creeping in for the kill. The coyote was intent on having Sherman for his dinner.

A large bobcat had also picked up Sherman's scent and was also closing in on Sherman. Poor Sherman was concentrating so hard on the coyote, he was totally unaware of the bobcat's presence.

The coyote was only a few feet

away now. Sherman knew that if it came any closer, he would have to take off running. He knew, too, that it would do no good to run, for there was no way he could outrun the coyote.

Sherman tensed up, ready to bolt and run. The bobcat was inching up behind Sherman. But still, Sherman hadn't noticed him. The coyote was now too close for comfort, and Sherman knew he had to run.

The coyote and the bobcat reached young Sherman just as he sprang to his feet and darted through the forest. They both pounced. They pounced on the very spot where Sherman had been lying! They fought over who was going to have lamb for dinner.

As the two fought, Sherman ran as fast as he could. He could hear the yelps of the coyote and the cries of the bobcat. They were fighting a terrible fight!

Sherman was running so fast when he reached the creek, he couldn't stop. He flew right out into the middle of the creek.

Sherman struggled, trying to get to the bank, but it was no use. He couldn't swim.

Sherman kept struggling and

finally managed to reach the creek bank on the other side. When he got

out of the creek, he ran as fast as he could run. He ran up the creek bank for a long way.

Sherman noticed he couldn't hear the coyote or the bobcat anymore. He thought they were hot on his trail.

What Sherman didn't know was that the bobcat had won the fight but had lost Sherman's trail at the creek.

Sherman came into a small clearing. He stopped when he saw a bridge crossing the creek. He remembered crossing that bridge on the way to the summer pasture.

Sherman called out, then ran across the bridge. He ran until he reached the flock. They were nestled together in the middle of the pasture. He walked through the flock of sheep, sniffing. Finally, he smelled his mama. He curled up beside her.

As Sherman lay beside his mama, he said to himself, "I'm never going to pout and cry again when I don't get my way. I know now that my mama is a good teacher, and she knows best."

Four

Sheep Facts

Sheep are hollow-horned ruminants or cud-chewers. They are similar to goats but have stockier bodies, scent glands in their faces and hind feet, and the males do not have beards.

Domesticated sheep are also more timid and prefer to flock and

follow a leader. Large wild sheep with spiral horns occur in several areas of the world and are frequently hunted for trophies. One of these is the argali, found in Central Asia and the Altai Mountains.

Rocky Mountain bighorn sheep are found in higher elevations from Mexico to Alaska. They are typically a brownish tan color, but color ranges from the almost white to an almost black.

The worldwide population of sheep is estimated at about one billion. Major sheep-raising countries include New Zealand, Australia, China, India, and the Central Asian republics.

Mutton and lamb are eaten in most of the countries where they are raised, but consumption in the U.S. has fallen to one pound per person per year.

U.S. sheep are raised primarily for their wool. It is the major commercial product of the sheep industry. Wool types are fine-wool, medium-wool white-face, and medium-wool dark-face. These breeds are also noted for their mutton qualities.

The thick, curly wool that forms a sheep's fleece can have blowflies and lice. Sheep dip, a liquid pesticide is used, but the dip is expensive, and may taint both wool and meat.

Sheared fleece is called "grease wool." Washing it removes the oil and lanolin, which is widely used in cosmetics.

About eleven and one-half million head of sheep are raised annually in the U.S. The leading states are Texas, California, Wyoming, and Colorado, where large flocks of 1,000 or more sheep, raised for wool, are grazed together. They are kept penned only for winter feeding and spring lambing.